Stories of
Knights

Retold by
Jane Bingham

Illustrated by
Alan Marks

Reading Consultant: Alison Kelly
University of Surrey Roehampton

Contents

Chapter 1

Sir Gawain and the Green Knight

It was New Year's Eve in the kingdom of Camelot and King Arthur was holding a feast. Everyone was eating, laughing and having fun when...

...a giant knight strode into the hall. He was as big as a bear and looked as wild as a wolf. But the strangest thing about him was – he was completely green.

The giant looked at King Arthur's knights, seated around the table.

After a pause, he roared, "Which of you will play a New Year's game with me?"

You chop off my head, then I'll chop off yours!

No one wanted to play his game. But the Green Knight refused to leave. Finally, Sir Gawain agreed. Seizing the giant's massive sword, he sliced off his green head.

Everyone gasped as the head bounced down the hall like a huge green ball.

Then the Green Knight's body calmly bent down, picked up the head and tucked it under his arm.

7

The head looked up. "Well done, Sir Gawain!" it said. "Now it's my turn."

Sir Gawain turned pale.

"You have a year and a day," the head went on. "Meet me at the Green Chapel next New Year's Day."

But where's the Green Chapel?

You must find it yourself.

The following winter, Sir Gawain set off. He knew he was riding to certain death but he had given his word.

He searched the kingdom with no success. By Christmas he was exhausted, but he would not give up.

9

At last, Sir Gawain came to a castle in a forest, owned by the lord Sir Bertilak. Sir Gawain asked his question and Sir Bertilak smiled.

"The Green Chapel?" he said. "It's just around the corner."

When Sir Bertilak heard Sir Gawain's story, he asked the knight to stay with him. For three days, Sir Bertilak went out hunting. Gawain stayed at home with Bertilak's wife.

Have a good day!

In the evenings, they ate dinner together. The knights told each other everything they had done during the day.

"I chased a stag!" said Bertilak, on the first night.

Gawain blushed. "I read to your wife and she gave me a kiss," he said.

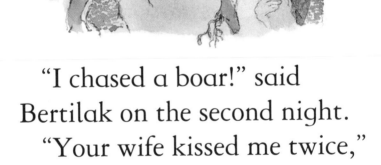

"I chased a boar!" said Bertilak on the second night.

"Your wife kissed me twice," said Gawain, bright red.

"I chased a fox!" said Bertilak on the third night.

"Your wife gave me three kisses," Gawain whispered.

But Gawain kept a secret. Sir Bertilak's wife had also given him a magic belt. She said it could save his life.

Gawain knew he should tell Bertilak. But he wanted to wear it when he met the Green Knight.

On New Year's Day, Sir Gawain rode to the Green Chapel. The Green Knight was waiting. Telling Gawain to kneel down, he raised his massive sword...

But then he lowered his sword again.

The Green
Knight raised
his sword for
a second time.
Again, he put
it down.

The third time he raised
his sword, Sir Gawain didn't
worry. But this time, the Green
Knight gave Gawain a painful
nick on the neck.

Why did you
do that?

The next minute, the giant
started to shrink...

and shrink...

until he
turned into…

…Sir Bertilak!

Huh?

"Yes!" cried Sir Bertilak. "I was the Green Knight. It was a test. I know you're brave because you came to seek me. But I wanted to see how honest a knight you were, too."

"So, I asked my wife to kiss you and give you the belt," Sir Bertilak went on. "Twice, you told me the truth and I didn't harm you. But the third time you kept a secret."

Sir Gawain fell to his knees. "I'm a bad knight," he said. "I'm a coward. You should cut off my head."

"Nonsense!" said Sir Bertilak. "You didn't do that badly. Now, come back to the castle. I've organized a feast."

No more games – I promise!

Chapter 2

The tale of the kitchen knight

One day, a young stranger arrived at King Arthur's castle. He had beautiful white hands but his clothes were old and torn.

19

"I have nowhere to go," he told the king. "Please Sire, may I stay for a year?"

King Arthur liked the look of him, so he agreed. "Sir Kay can take care of you," he said.

Grumpy Sir Kay was in charge of the kitchens. He sneered at the young boy. "Hmph! I shall call you Pretty Hands," he said. "Now, let's see how hard you can work."

Pretty Hands
stirred soup...

peeled
vegetables...

mopped
floors...

and washed
dishes.

He even
chopped
wood.
But he never complained.

When Pretty Hands had been at the castle for almost a year, a lady came to Camelot. Her name was Linnet and she was very rude.

"Get me a knight! I need help," she declared. "My sister Lyonesse has been captured by the Red Knight."

No one wanted to help Linnet. Then Pretty Hands stepped forward. "I'll rescue your sister," he announced.

Everyone was shocked. He was only the kitchen boy.

Lady Linnet was furious. "I want a real knight," she stormed, "not a boy who smells of the kitchen!"

"Don't worry, my Lady," said King Arthur. "Sir Lancelot will make him into a real knight first."

Just before he was knighted, Pretty Hands told Sir Lancelot a secret. His real name was Gareth and he was Sir Gawain's brother.

Arise, Sir Gareth!

The next day, Sir Gareth set off with Lady Linnet to rescue her sister. They faced dragons and worse. Gareth killed them all, but Linnet wasn't impressed.

At last, they reached the Red Knight's castle. Lady Lyonesse was locked in a tower. When she saw Sir Gareth she smiled. Gareth took one look at her and fell in love.

Fair lady, I promise I will set you free!

Gareth rode up to the castle and hammered on the door. There was a terrible roar. Then the door opened and the Red Knight thundered out.

Sir Gareth and the Red Knight fought for hours. It was a hard battle and both of them were badly wounded. But, as the sun sank and the stars rose, Sir Gareth finally won.

Leaving the Red Knight on the ground, Gareth raced to the tower and unlocked Lady Lyonesse. Before she could say a word, he asked her to marry him.

Back at Camelot, King Arthur gave the couple a grand wedding. When Gareth told him his real name, he was welcomed to the Round Table to sit beside his brother.

"Not bad – for a kitchen boy!" said Lady Linnet.

Chapter 3

Sir Gawain and the Loathly Lady

But you said you loved *me*!

Sir Gawain liked pretty girls, but sometimes he made them cry. So Arthur's wife, Queen Guinevere, decided to teach him a lesson.

She asked Gawain an impossible question and told him to return in a year and a day with the answer.

If he was right, she would hold a feast for him. But if he was wrong, she would ask Arthur to chop off his head.

Sir Gawain rode all over the kingdom. He asked every woman he met exactly the same question. But each one gave him a different answer.

After a year, Sir Gawain still had no idea what women really wanted. He rode back to Camelot, dreading what Guinevere would say.

On the way, he passed some beautiful dancers in a forest. But as he drew near, they vanished.

In their place stood an old woman. Sir Gawain decided to ask her his question.

When she turned around to reply, he nearly screamed out loud.

She was the ugliest creature he had ever seen.

She's hideous! What a loathly lady!

One of her eyes looked up at the sky. The other looked down to the ground. Her long nose was bent to one side and her face was covered in pimples.

The Loathly Lady gave Sir Gawain a ghastly grin. "I can answer your question," she cackled. "But in return you must do something for me."

Sir Gawain agreed. "I'll come back as soon as I've seen Queen Guinevere."

The answer to your question is...

Gawain galloped all the way to Camelot. When he reached the castle, he marched up to the queen and gave her his answer.

"Your majesty, the thing women really want is…" He paused.

What do you think he'll say?

Shh! I want to hear.

"...to have their own way," he finished. Queen Guinevere smiled. Then all the women in the hall smiled as well.

That's it!

How did he guess?

Sir Gawain had passed the
test! But while everyone else
enjoyed the queen's party, he
rode back to the forest. There,
he asked the Loathly Lady
what she wanted him
to do.

Sir Gawain turned white.
But he had given his word.

Sir Gawain and the Loathly Lady were married the same day. That night, the Loathly Lady turned to her husband.

"I can be both beautiful and ugly," she told him, "but you have to choose."

"Do you want me fair by night and foul by day?"

"Or foul by night and fair by day?"

Sir Gawain knew exactly what he wanted, but then he remembered what he had learned. "Dear wife," he said, "you must choose. I want you to have your own way."

When she heard his answer, the Loathly Lady smiled. Gawain gasped. She was no longer an ugly old hag...

...but a beautiful girl.

"Dear Gawain!" she cried.
"I was under a spell. But your
kindness has set me free."

This is who I really
am – and how I'll stay
from now on!

The Legend of King Arthur

Tales about King Arthur and his knights first appeared hundreds of years ago, in a book called "The History of the Kings of Britain" by Geoffrey of Monmouth. It was called a history book but he probably made most of it up.

Later, stories about Arthur were retold by French writers and the legend spread through Europe. Then an English knight named Thomas Malory translated the French tales back into English. He put the tales in a long book but gave it a French title, "Le Morte d'Arthur" (The Death of Arthur). The stories in here are based on Sir Malory's book.

Series editor: Lesley Sims

Designed by
Russell Punter

First published in 2004 by Usborne Publishing Ltd., Usborne House,
83-85 Saffron Hill, London EC1N 8RT, England. www.usborne.com
Copyright © 2004 Usborne Publishing Ltd.